THE TIME WARP WONDER

Don't miss any of the cases in the Hardy Boys Clue Book series!

HARDY BOYS

→Clue Book←

#8

THE TIME WARP WONDER

BY FRANKLIN W. DIXON ⟷ ILLUSTRATED BY SANTY GUTIÉRREZ

ALADDIN

NEW YORK   LONDON   TORONTO   SYDNEY   NEW DELHI

ALADDIN

An imprint of Simon & Schuster Children's Publishing Division
1230 Avenue of the Americas, New York, NY 10020
First Aladdin paperback edition November 2018
Text copyright © 2018 by Simon & Schuster, Inc.
Illustrations copyright © 2018 by Santy Gutiérrez
Also available in an Aladdin hardcover edition.

For information about special discounts for bulk purchases, please contact
Simon & Schuster Special Sales at 1-866-506-1949 or business@simonandschuster.com.
The Simon & Schuster Speakers Bureau can bring authors to your live event.
For more information or to book an event contact the Simon & Schuster Speakers Bureau
at 1-866-248-3049 or visit our website at www.simonspeakers.com.
Series designed by Karina Granda
Cover designed by Nina Simoneaux
The text of this book was set in Adobe Garamond Pro.
Manufactured in the United States of America 1018 OFF
2 4 6 8 10 9 7 5 3 1
Library of Congress Control Number 2017049432
ISBN 978-1-5344-1392-4 (hc)
ISBN 978-1-5344-1391-7 (pbk)
ISBN 978-1-5344-1393-1 (eBook)

CONTENTS

SCIENCE FAIR STANDOFF

"What's your science fair project, Joe?" Chet Morton asked. "It looks like a spaghetti strainer with bells on the sides."

Eight-year-old Joe Hardy proudly held up his project. It was a Friday in October. The third and fourth graders were setting up their projects for the Bayport Elementary School Science Fair. The fair would be held on Monday in the lunchroom.

"It may look like a spaghetti strainer to you, Chet," Joe told his friend. "But there's more to the Joe Hardy Lie Detector Helmet than meets the eye."

"Or eyes," Joe's nine-year-old brother, Frank, said. "Show Chet the chart you made, Joe."

Joe's chart showed two faces he'd drawn himself. Underneath one face was the word *Truth*. Underneath the other was *Lie*.

"The lying eyes look funny," Chet said. "How come?"

"A lie can make eyes shift back and forth," Joe explained, "which makes the muscles on the sides of the head move, which makes the bells on my lie detector helmet ring!"

"A lie detector helmet!" Chet exclaimed. "Awesome!"

"Give it a try, Chet," Frank suggested. "You've got nothing to hide."

Joe pointed to a stain on Chet's shirt and said, "Except the chocolate bar you snuck into class today!"

Chet rubbed the stain with his thumb. He loved

snacking more than anything else. He also loved trying out new things!

"Okay," Chet said. "Just don't ask me about the candy bar."

Joe helped Chet pull on the helmet. He waited for the bells to be still, then asked the first question. "Chet, yes or no: Is your favorite lunch at school macaroni and cheese?"

"A humongous yes!" Chet declared.

The bells on the helmet rang as his eyes darted back and forth.

"I don't get it, Chet," Frank said. "Everyone knows that mac and cheese is your favorite lunch."

"It is my favorite lunch," Chet said.

"So . . . why were your eyes bouncing back and forth like Ping-Pong balls?" Joe asked.

"Because we're in the lunchroom," Chet said. He pointed to a small blackboard listing next week's lunch menu. "I was looking to see if we're having mac and cheese on Monday!"

Chet sighed as he took off the helmet. "Veggie loaf instead. Boring."

"Don't you want me to ask more questions?" Joe asked.

"I want to try out Frank's project next," said Chet. "I heard it's a detective science project too."

"Surprise, surprise," Joe said with a smile.

The Hardy brothers were detectives and were always ready for a mystery. That was why Joe never left the house without their clue book. The book was where Joe and Frank listed all their suspects and clues.

"Hey, wait a minute," said Frank as he sniffed the air. "I think I smell something cheesy right now."

"That's my science project," Chet said. "Follow me!"

Frank and Joe followed Chet through a crowd of students setting up their projects. The school science teacher, Ms. Klinger, was there to approve the projects before the fair.

Chet brought the brothers to a table against the wall. On it was a plate covered with a dome-shaped lid.

"Ta-daaa!" Chet announced as he pulled up the

lid to reveal a pizza slice. "Introducing the Chet Morton Pizza Project!"

"Now it's my lunch!" a voice sneered as a hand yanked the slice off the plate.

"Hey!" Chet complained.

Frank, Joe, and Chet turned to see a tall boy holding the slice above his gaping mouth. It was fourth grader Adam Ackerman—the biggest bully at Bayport Elementary.

"Put it down, Adam," Frank insisted.

"I will!" Adam snickered. "Down the hatch!"

Adam was about to take a bite when he frowned. "I don't see any toppings on this slice. Where's the pepperoni? The mushrooms? The anchovies?"

"Anchovies?" Joe said, wrinkling his nose. "Who eats hairy little fish on their pizza?"

Adam glared at Joe. "I like hairy little fish on my pizza, Hardy!" he snapped. "Got a problem with that?"

Joe was about to answer when Chet piped up: "But it does have toppings, Adam. Fuzzy green moldy toppings!"

Adam stared at the slice. "Moldy?" He gulped.

"It's my science project," Chet explained. "I want to see how long it takes a slice of pizza to rot."

"In fact," said Joe, tilting his head, "I think I see some green stuff on it already!"

"*Bon appétit*, Ackerman," Frank said.

Adam's face burned red as he slammed the pizza slice back down onto the plate. "Who ever heard of a pizza science project?" he muttered.

"At least I have a science project, Ackerman!"

Chet shouted after Adam as the bully stormed away.

"You tell him, Chet," said Joe. "The only thing Adam has down to a science is acting like a creep."

Frank examined the pizza on the plate. "There's no mold on it yet," he pointed out. "How long does it take for pizza to get funky, Chet?"

"I don't know," Chet said with a shrug. "I've never left pizza uneaten long enough to find out!"

He was about to put the lid back, when—

"Eeeeek!"

Racing through the room with her hands in the air was Mrs. Carmichael, the lunch lady!

"A mouse is running through my clean lunchroom!" Mrs. Carmichael shouted as she ran. "Somebody call the custodian to catch the little pest!"

Joe pointed in the direction of a furry little creature. It was climbing on top of Daisy Zamora's solar-system diorama.

"There's the mouse!" he declared.

The creature hopped off the diorama and dashed straight toward Perry Lichtenstein's baking-soda volcano.

Iola Morton, Chet's sister, charged toward the volcano. "Come back!" she shouted. "Please, come back!"

"Hey, Chet," Frank asked. "Why is Iola chasing a mouse?"

"Because that's no mouse!" Chet said, his eyes wide. "That's Crusty!"

Chapter 2

TIME WARPED

"You mean Crusty, your pet hamster?" Frank asked Chet.

"Yeah, he's the star of Iola's science project," Chet explained.

"What kind of project?" asked Joe.

"Iola's proving that a hamster will run through a maze to get veggies on the other side," Chet said.

Crusty hopped from one table to the next until he landed on the one with Chet's pizza project. The little brown hamster with the white spot on his stomach nibbled hungrily at the slice.

"Looks like Crusty would rather eat pizza than veggies," Joe said, pointing.

"That's why we named him Crusty!" said Chet. "His favorite part of the slice is the crust!"

Iola smiled as she picked up Crusty. She turned to Mrs. Carmichael and said, "Crusty's not a mouse. Just a cute little hamster."

"I don't care if he's a magic unicorn," Mrs. Carmichael snapped. "No critters in my clean lunchroom."

"Crusty is my science project, Mrs. Carmichael," Iola explained. "I'll make sure he doesn't escape from his carrier again."

"How did Crusty escape from his carrier?" Chet asked his sister. "Did you leave the door open?"

"Just a crack," Iola admitted. "I didn't want him to feel trapped, since he's in a new place. I brought him today so he could get used to the lunchroom for Monday."

"You want him to feel at home? Take him there!" Mrs. Carmichael demanded.

The rubber soles on Mrs. Carmichael's shoes squeaked as she headed back to the kitchen.

"Definitely not a hamster fan," Joe said.

"She's not," a voice declared, "but I am!"

The boys and Iola turned to see Trent Greengrass hurrying over. Trent was in Frank's fourth-grade class.

"You like hamsters, Trent?" asked Frank.

"Totally," Trent said with a smile. "If I had my own hamster, I'd enter him in those cool hamster ball races."

"Hamster ball races?" Iola asked.

"What are those?" Joe wanted to know.

"It's where hamsters are put inside clear plastic balls," Trent explained. "When the hamsters run, the balls roll around."

"Pretty cool," Frank admitted.

"That's why I want to borrow that hamster," said Trent, pointing to Crusty, "so I can enter him in those races."

"Borrow him?" Chet asked.

"Crusty is our pet, Trent," Iola said. "We don't just lend him out like a library book."

"Besides, Crusty's had enough racing for now," said Chet, "through the whole lunchroom!"

Trent's shoulders slumped. He muttered, "Whatever," before trudging away.

"I'd better put Crusty back into his carrier," Iola said. "And this time I'm closing the door!"

"And I'm covering my pizza," Chet said as he placed

the dome-shaped lid over the slice, "just in case."

Frank, Joe, and Chet walked around the lunchroom to check out more science projects. They found their friend Phil Cohen standing next to a towering object shaped like a capsule. The whole thing was covered with silver foil from top to bottom.

"What's that, Phil?" asked Joe.

"It looks like a giant baked potato," Chet said.

Phil waved dramatically at his project. "Guys," he said, "meet the Phil Cohen Time Warp Wonder!"

"Time Warp Wonder?" Frank repeated.

"Dude," Joe said excitedly, "did you invent a time machine?"

Before Phil could answer, Ms. Klinger walked over. "Did someone say this is a time machine?" she asked with a smile.

"It is, Ms. Klinger," Phil said proudly. He nodded toward a plastic wheel. It had an arrow pointing to different time periods in history. "That wheel controls where in time you go."

Ms. Klinger tapped her chin thoughtfully as she studied Phil's time machine. "You're an excellent

inventor, Philip," she said, "but calling this a time machine might not be enough."

"Not enough?" Phil asked. "Why, Ms. Klinger?"

"You should show what makes it a time machine," said Ms. Klinger. "And if anyone can do it, it's you, Philip!"

Ms. Klinger walked on to the next project. When

she was out of earshot, Frank asked, "What are you going to do, Phil?"

"I don't know," Phil admitted. "How can I prove that my time machine is a time machine?"

"Uh . . . by sending someone back in time?" Joe suggested.

"I'll go first!" Chet said, stepping forward. "Send me back to the time of King Arthur."

"So you can sit around King Arthur's Round Table," asked Frank, "with his knights?"

Chet shook his head. "So I can sit around his table with all that food," he said. "I heard you could eat with your hands back then."

Suddenly—

"Are you still talking about food, Morton?"

Joe groaned at the familiar voice. It was Adam Ackerman—again!

"What's that?" Adam asked, pointing to Phil's science project. "A giant baked potato?"

"It's a time machine," Phil muttered.

"Chet was going to try it out," Joe piped up. "But I have a better idea."

"What?" asked Adam.

"Let's send you back in time instead, Adam," Joe joked, "and leave you there!"

"Hardy-har-har!" Adam said through gritted teeth. "I have an idea too!" He turned and dashed off.

"Where's he going?" Chet asked.

In a flash, Adam returned with something small and furry in his hands. It was Crusty!

"Give him back, Ackerman!" Iola shouted as she ran behind Adam. "I said, give him back!"

"What are you doing with our hamster, Adam?" Chet demanded.

Adam stepped toward Phil's time machine. "I'm sure they had hamsters back in the prehistoric age," he said. "They were called dino chow!"

Before anyone could stop him, Adam opened one of the time machine's doors. Squeezing into the time machine, he placed Crusty on a stool that was inside. With a grin, he stepped out and shut the door behind him.

Frank and Joe tried to grab the door handle. But Adam stood in front, arms folded across his chest.

"Show us how your time machine works, genius," Adam told Phil. "Unless it doesn't."

"Don't listen to him, Phil," said Frank.

"Yeah," Joe agreed. "You don't have to prove anything."

"Yes, I do," Phil insisted.

Using both hands, he turned the control wheel until the arrow pointed to *The Prehistoric Age*. He then tapped a green button marked *GO*.

"This is crazy," Frank said, shaking his head. "Nothing is going to—"

PFFFSSSSSSS!!

Frank, Joe, Chet, and Iola froze.

A thick pink mist oozed out from under the time machine. Bright lights began flashing on and off.

"Whoa!" Joe gasped.

Soon Phil's time machine was totally covered by the pink mist. So were the boys and Iola!

"Smells like strawberry shortcake!" Chet's voice declared.

About a minute passed before the mist began to clear. Through it, Frank and Joe saw more kids

watching the time machine. They also saw Adam Ackerman racing out of the lunchroom!

"Where's he going so fast?" Frank asked.

"Doesn't Adam want to see if Phil's time machine worked?" added Joe.

"It better not have worked!" Iola said angrily. "I don't want Crusty back in the days of dinosaurs. I want him here now."

"Go ahead, Phil," Chet said, nodding at the time machine. "Open the door and give us back our hamster."

Phil opened the door and peeked inside. "Um . . . I can't," he said. "I can't give you back your hamster."

"Why not?" asked Chet.

"Because," Phil said, opening the door wide, "Crusty is gone!"

Chapter 3

HAMSTER JAM

"Did you say 'gone'?" Chet asked Phil.

"How could he be gone?" Iola said. "The door was closed, wasn't it?"

The boys and Iola looked through the door into the time machine. The stool where Crusty had once sat was empty.

Frank stepped inside the time machine. He looked up, down, and all around. Joe looked inside too. There was no hamster anywhere.

21

"Wow!" Joe exclaimed. "You mean Crusty really went back in time?"

"Sure he did," Phil said. "What do you think I invent? Junk?"

"Okay," said Chet nervously. "Now turn the wheel and bring Crusty back to the twenty-first century."

"Yeah," Iola said. "I need him for my own science project!"

Phil stared at the time machine. "Um . . . sure, I'll bring Crusty back," he said. "As soon as I figure out how."

"What do you mean, 'figure out'?" Chet asked.

"My time machine is a work in progress!" Phil explained. "I have until Monday's science fair to work on it."

He turned to close the time machine door. Joe noticed something sticking out of the pocket of Phil's hoodie. Was that a little furry paw?

Just then Ms. Klinger made an announcement. "Boys and girls, I was very impressed with your projects. Go back to your classrooms, and then have a wonderful weekend. I'll see you here on Monday morning for the Bayport Elementary School Science Fair!"

Cheers filled the lunchroom.

Joe looked back at Phil's hoodie to ask him about that paw, but nothing was there. It didn't seem like anything was in his pocket anymore. Joe shook his head. Maybe he had imagined it.

"Figure out how to get our hamster back, Phil," Chet said firmly.

"And do it before Monday," added Iola.

Chet and Iola turned and walked away. After a quick good-bye to Frank and Joe, Phil walked away too.

"Awkward," Frank sighed.

"Do you think Crusty went back in time, Frank?" Joe asked.

Frank shook his head. "Even if Crusty did go back in time," he said, "why didn't Phil's time machine go with him?"

"It's the magic of science," Joe figured. "What else could it be?"

"The time machine was covered with all that

mist," said Frank. "I think someone opened the door during that time and took Crusty out."

"But going back in time would be awesome," Joe insisted. "I don't want to stop believing in that."

"You do want Chet and Phil to be friends again, right?" Frank asked.

Joe thought about it. Chet and Phil were their best friends. Having best friends fight was never cool.

"In that case," Joe said, "say hello to my little friend."

He pulled their clue book out of his pocket and said, "The science fair may be Monday, but we have another project to work on."

"Yeah," said Frank. "To find out what happened to Crusty!"

"A hot bowl of chili always says 'fall' to me," Laura Hardy said with a smile.

"To me it says 'yummo,'" Joe told his mother. "Winter, spring, summer, and fall."

It was Friday night. For the Hardy family, that meant dinner at Chuck Wagon Chili in Bayport.

While they waited for their order, Joe studied the clue book.

"We've got to put together a suspect list, Frank," he said.

"Let's start with the five *W*s," Frank suggested.

"Good call." Joe flipped to a new page and wrote them out:

The Five Ws.

1. Who
2. What
3. Where
4. When
5. Why

"We already know the *where* and the *when*," said Frank.

"Yup. In the lunchroom, this afternoon," Joe said as he wrote both answers down.

"Just need to know what happened to Crusty, who took him, and why." Frank scratched his head as he thought.

"Who do you think made Crusty disappear from the time machine?" Joe asked him.

"We did see Adam running out of the lunchroom," Frank pointed out. "Maybe he was running away with Crusty?"

"I thought Adam wanted Phil's project to fail," replied Joe. "Why would he want to make it look like Crusty had gone back in time?"

Frank was about to answer when their dad, Fenton Hardy, piped up. "Come on, guys. You know the deal. No electronics or clue book at the dinner table."

The brothers looked up from their clue book. Their dad was a private investigator and often helped them with their cases. As long as it was not at the dinner table!

"But dinner isn't ready yet, Dad," Joe said. "They have to call our number first. Then Frank and I go to the counter to pick up our chili."

"It's not a number, Joe," Frank said. "You know that every table here is named after a famous cowboy or cowgirl."

"Wyatt Earp!" a voice shouted over the loudspeaker. "Come rustle up yer grub!"

"Yee-haw, that's us!" Joe said, closing the clue book. "Let's get it, Frank."

The owner of the chili place, Chuck, stood behind the counter. As the brothers approached, they saw someone else.

"Trent Greengrass is picking up food," Joe said. "Let's say hi."

Frank put his hand on his brother's arm. "Wait!" he whispered. "Didn't Trent want to borrow Crusty—to enter some of those hamster races?"

"He did!" Joe whispered back.

Frank and Joe stood a few feet behind Trent while he grabbed his take-out bag. They could hear every word. . . .

"Here you go, cowboy!" Chuck said. "Don't tell me you're fixin' to down all those smoked ribs by yourself?"

Trent nodded and said, "I need a lot of energy tomorrow, Chuck."

"Are you playing soccer?" asked Chuck.

"Better than soccer," Trent said. "It's the Hamster Ball Relay Race tomorrow!"

"Well, good luck, cowboy!" Chuck said with a smile.

Trent was too busy counting his change to notice Frank and Joe as he left the chili place.

"Frank," Joe said slowly, "did you just hear what I just heard?"

Chapter 4

ON A ROLL

"So Trent is going to a hamster race tomorrow," Frank said softly.

"And what does a guy need for a hamster race?" Joe asked. "A hamster like Crusty."

"We know Trent wanted to borrow Crusty," Frank said. "But I didn't see him near Phil's time machine this afternoon."

"With all that misty stuff, we could hardly see

anyone!" Joe said. "I say Trent Greengrass is a suspect!"

"And I say pick up your chili before it gets cold, Wyatt Earp!" called Chuck.

"Oh, right," Joe said, hurrying over to the counter. "Sorry about that, Chuck."

He and Frank picked up two trays filled with chili bowls, corn bread, and iced teas. They stopped at a counter for straws, spoons, and napkins on their way to the table.

"Should we find out where Trent lives?" Joe asked, grabbing a handful of straws. "So we can look for Crusty tomorrow?"

Frank was looking up at a bulletin board above the counter. "I know where to find Trent tomorrow," he said.

"Where?" Joe asked.

"There!" said Frank as he pointed at a flyer. In big letters it read: HAMSTER BALL RELAY! BAYPORT PARK! SATURDAY AT 11:00!

"That's got to be the race Trent told Chuck about," Joe said, "where hamsters run inside little balls."

"If that's where Trent will be tomorrow," Frank said, "then that's where we'll be!"

The next morning, before they headed out, Frank and Joe wrote a suspect list consisting of Trent and Adam. They told Aunt Trudy where they were going and left the Hardy house with a plan: they would find Trent at the Hamster Ball Relay. Then they would demand to see Crusty.

"It's a good thing you saw that flyer last night, Frank," Joe said as they walked out their front door.

"Speaking of flyers," Frank said, pointing to a nearby tree, "there's another one in our yard."

"That's a weird place for it," said Joe with a frown. "Not many people would see a flyer in our yard, would they?"

The brothers stepped up to the tree. There was a piece of paper taped to the trunk, but it wasn't a flyer.

"It's a picture of a hamster," Joe said as he pulled the picture off the tree. He and Frank studied it closely.

"How weird is that?" Frank said. "The hamster

in the picture is wearing a leopard-print robe—and he's holding a club just like a caveman."

"And look at all those dinosaurs behind him, Frank," Joe said. "I have a feeling Crusty isn't rolling in the hamster race today."

"Then where is he?" Frank asked.

"He's back in the prehistoric age," Joe exclaimed, "rolling with dinosaurs!"

"No way, Joe," said Frank. "Whoever took Crusty is just trying to be funny."

"Funny?" Joe asked as he folded the picture and slipped it into his pocket. "Nothing funny about being chased by dinosaurs!"

At the park, Frank and Joe saw no signs of a Hamster Ball Relay. There were no hamster balls or even hamsters!

"Where do you think the race is?" Frank asked.

Joe spotted a crowd in the near distance. They all seemed to be watching something. Some were holding up their phones to take pictures.

"They must be watching the race," Joe said with a smile. "Let's see if we can find Trent."

Frank and Joe squeezed through the crowd until an open field came into view. Rolling across the lawn were giant clear balls. Inside the balls, making them roll, were kids. Human kids!

"It *is* going to be a hamster ball race," Frank groaned. "A human hamster ball race!"

The brothers watched people warm up for the race. Up ahead, a long ribbon was hung across the field. Clearly that was the starting line. They could see Trent in one of the balls lined up behind it.

"Why would Trent need Crusty for a race like this?" Joe asked.

"He wouldn't," Frank sighed. "Come on, Joe. Let's go home."

"Wait!" said Joe. "Just because Trent is in a human hamster ball race today doesn't mean he won't race a real live hamster tomorrow!"

Before his brother could stop him, Joe sped across the field to Trent's human hamster ball.

"Trent, listen up!" he shouted through the thick plastic. "Did you take Chet's hamster out of Phil's time machine?"

Trent pointed to both ears. "I can't hear you," he mouthed.

"Great," Joe muttered.

He was about to turn away, when he spotted something. On the side of the hamster ball was a large flap. Joe lifted the flap and found a hole—big enough for a kid to squeeze through.

"What are you doing?" Trent cried as Joe squeezed through the hole into the giant ball.

"Trying to find out what happened to Crusty," Joe replied. He stood up but stumbled as Trent began rolling.

"Joe, get out now!" Trent said.

"Why?" Joe asked, trying to run in place. "Because you don't want to tell me where Crusty is?"

"No!" Trent shouted back. "Because we're about to race!"

"Huh?" Joe cried. The next words he heard were: "On your mark . . . get set . . . roll!"

Chapter 5

SIR HAMSTERLOT

"Whooooaaaa!" Joe cried.

Trent was rolling the giant hamster ball—and them—down a long inflatable racing track.

"Go, Trent and Joe!" Frank cheered from the crowd.

Joe got into it as he shouted, "We got this, Green-grass! We got this!"

Trent and Joe gave their hamster ball one last shove toward the finish line. The crowd went wild as their hamster ball rolled into first place!

Joe crawled out through the hole, followed by Trent. When they were both on their feet, they high-fived.

"First place, dude!" Trent cheered.

"Break it down," Joe shouted. "Break it—"

"Excuse me, boys," a voice interrupted.

The boys turned to see a man. He wore a serious expression on his face and a plastic ID around his neck: HARVEY VICKERS, HAMSTER BALL RELAY JUDGE.

"I'm afraid you're not the winners," Mr. Vickers said.

"Why not?" Trent asked.

"Only one person to a hamster ball," Mr. Vickers explained. "Those are the rules."

Joe felt awful. Trent had been disqualified because of him. But before he could apologize—

"And the winner of the human Hamster Ball Relay is," the announcer boomed, "Daisy Zamora!"

"Woo-hooooo!" Daisy shouted, jumping up and down next to her hamster ball. "Free garlic knots for everybody at my parents' pizza place!"

Frank came over just as Trent began walking away.

"Sorry, Trent," Joe called. "I only wanted to find out about Crusty."

"I never took that hamster!" Trent insisted.

"Then where were you yesterday," asked Frank, "when Phil's time machine oozed all that misty stuff?"

Trent stopped walking and turned around. "You mean this?" he asked.

He pulled a phone from his pocket and held it up to show the brothers a video. It was of Phil's time machine covered with mist!

"It was so awesome that I had to get a video," Trent explained. "Maybe I'll put it on YouTube."

Frank and Joe watched the video. Phil's time machine seemed to be at least ten feet away from Trent.

"So you were all the way on the other side of the lunchroom when Phil's time machine started?" Joe asked.

"Just about," said Trent.

"If you were recording it from over there," Frank

said, "you couldn't have taken Crusty out of the time machine."

"I told you," Trent sighed, "I didn't take the hamster!"

Joe believed Trent. He also believed that Trent's video could be a great clue!

"Play the video to the end, Trent," Joe said. "Maybe we'll see who really took Crusty."

"That's all I have," Trent said after the video stopped. "Ms. Klinger made me quit filming. No phones in the lunchroom. Ever."

Frank looked at Joe. He was pretty sure his brother was thinking the same thing he was. Trent may have wanted a hamster—but not bad enough to take one from Chet.

"Sorry for thinking you took Crusty, Trent," Frank said.

"It's okay," said Trent. "You guys were only being detectives."

"And I was being a jerk, crawling into your hamster ball," Joe admitted. "You lost the race because of me."

"That's okay too," Trent said. "I signed up for two more hamster ball races today."

"Two more?" Joe exclaimed.

"Sure," Trent said with a grin. "I guess you can say I'm on a roll!"

Trent left to return to his human hamster ball. Frank and Joe crunched over dry leaves as they walked out of the park.

"These leaves remind me," Frank said. "We promised Mom and Dad we'd rake the yard today."

"I'd rather work on the case," said Joe. He took out the clue book and crossed Trent's name off the suspect list.

Frank looked over Joe's shoulder at the page. "The only suspect left is Adam," he said. "We'll have to talk to him about Crusty."

"Talk to Adam Ackerman?" Joe groaned. "Come to think of it, I'd rather rake leaves."

Frank and Joe had fun kicking and tossing leaves all the way home. After eating grilled cheese sandwiches for lunch, they got to work raking the front yard.

"Hey, Frank," Joe said, adding leaves to his pile. "What if Crusty really did go back in time?"

"Give me a break," Frank sighed as he raked. "Do you really still believe that?"

"Why not?" Joe said. "Phil is an awesome inventor, so why couldn't he invent a time machine that worked?"

Frank stopped raking. "Shh," he said in a low voice. "Did you hear that?"

"Hear what?" asked Joe.

"I heard some rustling," Frank said, "over by the hedges."

Joe looked over at the hedges separating the yard from the sidewalk. "It's probably just a squirrel," he said.

"Joe, look!" said Frank. He pointed to the garage. Projected onto the door was a picture of a hamster dressed in knight armor. Behind the hamster were human knights riding on horseback!

"Whoa!" Joe gasped.

The brothers dropped their rakes to approach the picture. It just about covered the whole garage door.

"What's a hamster doing dressed like a knight?" Frank asked.

"That's not just any hamster. It's Crusty!" Joe said. "And now he's in the Middle Ages, about five hundred years ago!"

The picture suddenly disappeared. Almost right away Frank and Joe heard more rustling noises.

"Whoever projected that picture must be hiding," Frank said. He waved his hand in the direction of the hedges. "Come on, Joe!"

The brothers raced across the yard to the hedges. But when they looked over them . . .

"No one's there," said Joe.

They looked up and down the sidewalk. No one was running away, either.

"Maybe it was a squirrel," Frank said.

"A squirrel in the bushes," Joe said, "and a hamster back in King Arthur's court!"

"Joe, I told you," Frank groaned. "Whoever took Crusty is just messing with us."

"I know how we can find out if that hamster was

Crusty," Joe said. "Did he have a white spot on his belly?"

"I couldn't see," said Frank. "He was holding a shield in front of his stomach."

Then he shook his head and said, "How does a hamster hold a shield with such little paws, anyway?"

Paws! Joe's eyes flashed as he remembered the paw sticking out of Phil's pocket. How had he not thought of that before?

"Forget about questioning Adam, Frank," Joe said. "I just thought of another suspect."

"Who?" Frank asked.

"You're not going to like it," said Joe with a frown, "but the suspect is Phil."

Chapter 6

POCKET SCIENCE

"Phil? Our friend Phil?" Frank exclaimed. "Why would he take Crusty?"

"I thought I saw something sticking out of his pocket," Joe said. "It looked just like a hamster paw that could have been Crusty's!"

"What was the paw doing?" Frank teased. "Waving bye-bye?"

Joe rolled his eyes. "I know we don't like accusing

friends," he said, "but maybe Phil wanted to make it look like his time machine worked. To get Adam to stop messing with him."

"Why wouldn't Phil tell us he had Crusty?" Frank asked. "Adam had already run out of the lunchroom."

"I don't know," Joe admitted. "I just know that I want to ask Phil about that paw."

"And have Phil think we don't trust him?" Frank asked. "Not cool."

He went back to raking leaves. Joe was about to scrap the idea, when another popped into his head. . . .

"Frank, remember when we tried out my lie detector helmet on Chet?" Joe asked. "Why don't we ask Phil to try it next?"

"I guess we could do that," said Frank. "We can ask some hamster questions and see if the bells ring or not."

"Awesome," Joe said with a smile. "Aren't you glad I remembered that paw in Phil's pocket?"

"Sure," Frank said. "Now if you could remember something else . . ."

"What?" asked Joe.

"Your chore," Frank said. "Pick up your rake and get to work!"

Joe quickly pulled out the suspect list and added Phil before getting back to work. The brothers finished raking the front yard and headed straight to the Cohen house. Joe carried his lie detector helmet.

"Phil has a Junior Inventors Club meeting every Saturday afternoon," Frank said on the way. "Maybe we can talk to him before it starts."

"It's a good thing I brought this home for the weekend, Frank," Joe said, tapping his lie detector helmet. "I wanted to polish the bells before the science fair on Monday."

"Polish the bells?" Frank asked with a grin. "Since when are you so neat?"

When they arrived at the Cohen house, Frank used the brass knocker to rap on the door. After a few seconds, Phil opened the door with a smile.

"What's that?" he asked, nodding at the helmet.

"It's a lie detector helmet," Joe answered.

"And Joe's project for the science fair," Frank added.

Phil raised an eyebrow. "So . . . why did you bring a lie detector here?"

"I want to try it out before Monday," Joe replied. "And who better to ask than the best inventor at school?"

Phil beamed at the compliment. "Okay, but make it speedy," he said. "My Junior Inventors Club will be here any minute."

Frank and Joe stepped into the entrance hall. Phil pulled the lie detector helmet onto his head and said, "What next?"

"Next I ask you some yes-or-no questions," Joe explained. "I promise the first question will be easy."

Joe waited until the bells on the helmet were still. He then asked, "Phil . . . do you have a hamster in your room?"

CLANG, CLANG, CLANG!

The bells on the helmet rang as Phil's eyes darted back and forth.

"I don't have a hamster," Phil said. "What kind of question is that?"

Joe and Frank traded sideways glances. If Phil didn't have a hamster, why were the lie detector bells ringing out of control?

"Next question," Frank piped up. "Do you own a hamster? As a pet?"

"No," Phil replied quickly.

This time the bells didn't ring.

"Then by any chance," asked Joe, "do you have someone else's hamster in your room?"

CLANG, CLANG, CLANG!

"Arrrgh!" Phil cried. He pulled off the helmet with the jangling bells. "What's with all the questions about hamsters? I don't want to do this anymore."

"But your club isn't here yet," Frank said.

"I promised to help my mom make snacks," Phil said, handing the helmet back to Joe. "You guys know the way out. I'll see you Monday."

As Phil headed toward the kitchen, Joe whispered, "We also know the way to Phil's room."

"What does that mean?" whispered Frank.

"It means," Joe whispered back, "it's time for a little hamster hunt."

Joe kept the bells from ringing as he and Frank climbed the stairs to Phil's room. It looked like a mad scientist's lab, filled with things Phil had invented.

Joe placed the lie detector helmet on Phil's desk. Then he and Frank searched the room for any hamster signs.

"I see a ton of gadgets and gizmos," Frank said, "but no hamster."

"I don't see any hamster stuff either," added Joe. "No hamster cage, toys, or bag of cedar chips—"

"Wait, Joe," Frank cut in. He pointed to a table against one of the walls. On it was something bulky covered with a white sheet.

"What do you think is under there?" he asked.

"I don't know," Joe said. "Let's check it out."

The brothers walked toward the table. When Joe saw something sticking out from under the sheet, he gulped.

"Frank . . . it's a paw!" he said. "The same hamster paw I saw in Phil's pocket."

"What's that whirring noise?" Frank asked. "We have to see what's underneath the sheet!"

He yanked the sheet away. Lying on the table was a hairy hamster with flashing red eyes!

"Holy cannoli!" Joe cried.

The hamster gave a sudden jerk. Frank and Joe jumped back as it rolled off the table onto the floor. It landed on both feet with a *CLUNK* before lumbering forward!

"Now I know what Phil did with Crusty," Joe shouted. "He created a Frankenhamster!"

Chapter 7

HAIRY SCARY

WHIRRRRRR! The Frankenhamster lumbered forward.

Frank and Joe were about to run out of the room, when Phil and more kids filed in. The brothers recognized some kids from the Junior Inventors Club.

"What are you doing in my room?" Phil asked.

Austin Ling, the nine-year-old president of the club, stepped forward. "And what are you doing with our latest invention?" he asked with a nod at the Frankenhamster.

"Invention, huh?" Joe snorted. "More like mad science!"

"Is that Crusty, Phil?" Frank asked. "What did you do with him?"

Phil pointed to the Frankenhamster. "Does that look like Crusty to you?" he asked. "That's Hammy, our robo-hamster."

"Robo-hamster?" Joe repeated.

"This project was supposed to be top secret," Austin said angrily. "How did you guys find out about it?"

"We're detectives," replied Frank. "It's our job to find out things."

Another club member, Allison Kernkraut from the third grade, stepped forward.

"And it's our job to invent awesome stuff," she said with a smile. "Hammy is for the annual Young Inventors Competition next month."

"Robo-hamsters don't need food or goofy hamster toys," Phil said. "Just double-A batteries."

"And you never have to clean out a yucky cage," Allison added. "That's the best part about owning a robo-hamster!"

A sudden *CLUNK* made the kids whirl around. Hammy had fallen onto his back, and his legs were kicking in the air.

"Hmm," Austin said. "We've got to work on that."

While the others tended to Hammy, Phil turned to Frank and Joe. "Is that why you guys were in my room?" he asked. "You thought I had taken Crusty?"

Joe didn't answer. He picked up his lie detector helmet and held it out to Phil. "Could you put this on, Phil?" he asked.

"Joe, what are you doing?" asked Frank. "We already asked Phil a bunch of questions."

"Not all the questions," Joe said.

"Okay, I'll do it," Phil said. "But only because it's a pretty neat invention."

The bells jangled as Phil pulled on the helmet. When they stopped ringing, Joe asked the first question: "I saw a little furry paw sticking out of your pocket yesterday. Was it Crusty's paw?"

"Nope," Phil said.

Frank and Joe waited for the bells to ring. They did not.

"Next question, Phil," Joe said. "Was that paw in your pocket Hammy's paw?"

"Yup!" Phil said with a smile.

The bells stayed silent. Phil was telling the truth.

"I made the paws myself out of papier-mâché!" Phil explained proudly. "I brought one to school to show Austin. After school we attached the paws to Hammy."

The bells remained silent. Phil was telling the truth again.

"I have no idea why Crusty was missing from my time machine," Phil said as he took off the helmet, "and I don't want Chet to be mad at me forever."

"We'll find Crusty, Phil," Joe promised. "Even if we have to travel back in your time machine!"

"Joe," Frank sighed.

The brothers thanked Phil and the Junior Inventors Club. After leaving the Cohen house, they began to walk home.

"We forgot to tell Phil about the weird hamster pictures we've been getting," Joe said.

"It's a good thing we didn't," Frank said. "Phil's club would think he really invented a time machine."

"What's so crazy about that?" Joe asked. He stopped walking to cross Phil's name off their suspect list. "Our only suspect now is Adam."

"We still don't have any clues that Adam took Crusty," Frank said. "Except that we saw him run out of the lunchroom."

"I can think of another clue," said Joe with a frown. "He's a bully!"

When he and Frank reached the Hardy house, they found a surprise on their doorstep. It was a pizza box!

"Pizza for dinner," Joe exclaimed. "Awesome!"

"Why would Mom and Dad leave it outside to get cold like that?" Frank asked.

Joe thought it was weird too, especially when he heard his parents' voices inside the house. "The delivery guy always rings the bell," he said. "So what's up?"

Frank opened the box. There was no pizza inside. But there was a sheet of paper taped to the inside of the lid.

"It's a picture," Frank said, peeling it off.

Joe looked at the photo and said, "It's like those old-timey pictures I see in my history books."

The photo showed a crowd of people. The men wore high hats. The women wore long dresses with wide skirts.

Frank pointed to a man standing behind a speaker's podium. "There's something else we see in our history books—a president!"

Joe recognized the president right away. "That's Abraham Lincoln!" he said.

But then he saw another surprise. Standing sideways in the crowd was a furry creature dressed in a coat and high hat.

"The guy behind the podium may be President Lincoln," Joe pointed out, "but the guy with the furry face and whiskers—is Crusty!"

Chapter 8

FETCHING FIND

Joe couldn't believe his eyes as he studied the picture. "Abraham Lincoln was president in the middle of the 1800s," he told Frank, "which means Crusty is back there now."

Joe counted his fingers as he did the math. "First Crusty was back in the days of dinosaurs, then in the Middle Ages, and now he's in the 1800s!"

"So?" Frank said.

"So Crusty is going forward in time!" Joe said

excitedly. "Soon he'll be back home with Chet and Iola!"

Frank looked to see if the hamster had a white spot. But his coat covered his stomach.

"Even if it is Crusty, where did he get all those clothes?" Frank asked. "I don't remember Phil having a tiny hamster wardrobe in his time machine."

"Then how do you explain the picture in the pizza box?" asked Joe.

"I told you a hundred times," Frank groaned. "The person who took Crusty is just messing with us."

"The person took all the pizza, too," Joe said, "with extra cheese and anchovies."

"How do you know the pizza had anchovies?" Frank asked.

Joe pointed to pieces of toppings stuck to the box. "See the hairy little fish?" he said. "Who likes those things on their pizza anyway?"

"Hey," Frank said slowly. "Didn't Adam tell us he likes anchovies on his pizza?"

Joe's eyes lit up. "Adam does like anchovies!" he declared. "If the pizza was his, so was the picture in the pizza box!"

"We're throwing this stinky thing away," said Frank, shutting the box. "Then, first thing tomorrow, we're finding Adam."

"What if Adam doesn't answer our questions?" Joe asked. "The pizza box can't be our only evidence."

Frank agreed, until he got an idea.

"You tried out your science project on Phil," he said with a grin. "I'm trying mine out on Adam Ackerman!"

"Are you sure it's October, Frank?" Joe asked. "It's almost as hot as summer."

"It's October for sure," said Frank. He pointed to someone's porch draped with cobwebs and paper spiders. "That's the third house with Halloween decorations we've seen this morning."

It was Sunday after breakfast as the brothers made their way to the Ackerman house. In Frank's hand was a Frisbee coated with powdered sugar.

"All that dusty stuff is making my nose tickle," Joe complained. "Why did you sugarcoat your Frisbee again?"

"Because I'm going to throw the Frisbee at Adam," Frank explained. "When Adam catches it, he'll leave his fingerprints all over the powdered sugar."

"Then what?" Joe asked.

"Then we run with the Frisbee to school," Frank explained, "and match Adam's fingerprints with the fingerprints on the time machine's door handle."

"Why do we need his fingerprints, Frank?" Joe asked.

"To match the door on the other side of the time machine. We know his fingerprints will be on the door on the side we were all facing when Crusty disappeared. But if Adam's fingerprints are on the door on the *other* side of the machine, then that means he snuck around to the other side when the mist was everywhere. And if we know that, then we know he took Crusty!"

"Wow. Good thinking, Frank. Only one issue; it's Sunday," Joe said. "Are you sure the school is open?"

"I know it's open for school clubs," said Frank. "Let's hope the lunchroom is open too, so we can get to Phil's time machine!"

Joe felt his stomach sink when they reached the Ackerman house. Meeting with the biggest school bully was never fun!

Frank rang the doorbell. No one answered.

"Maybe the Ackermans are in their backyard," he said. "It's a nice day."

"No day with Adam is a nice day, Frank," Joe muttered. "But let's check out the back."

Frank and Joe walked around the house. They slowed as they approached an open window.

"I think I hear Adam's voice," Frank whispered.

The window was low enough for the boys to look through. Inside the Ackermans' den were Adam and his friend Tony Riccio. Adam's back was toward the window as he sat at a computer station. Tony stood nearby, taking pictures of—

"A hamster!" Joe whispered.

The little hamster was wearing an astronaut helmet. He stood calmly on a stack of books while Tony took more pictures.

"That hamster can't belong to Adam," Frank whispered. "He just has two dogs."

"Woof!"

Frank and Joe turned away from the window. Standing behind them were two dalmatians.

"Two *big* dogs, Frank!" Joe gulped.

Joe tried to wave the dogs away, but it was too

late. They kept barking until Adam and Tony turned toward the window.

"Hey!" Adam growled when he saw Frank and Joe. "What are you doing here?"

"We're playing Frisbee!" Joe said as he grabbed the sugarcoated Frisbee from Frank. "Catch!"

"Joe, what are you doing?" Frank hissed.

"Getting Adam's fingerprints," Joe whispered.

He tossed the Frisbee, and it soared through the open window. So did the dogs!

"Woof, woof, woof!"

Adam caught the Frisbee. His dogs leaped all over him to get it!

"Hardys!" Adam shouted from under his persistent pets. "You'll be sorry!"

Chapter 9

SQUEEZE PLAY

"Come on, Joe," Frank said. "Let's go!"

The brothers raced away from the window. They froze when they saw Mrs. Ackerman carrying supermarket bags toward the house.

"Are you boys here to visit Adam?" she asked with a smile. "Why don't you come inside and surprise him?"

"Um . . . I think we already surprised him, Mrs. Ackerman," Joe said. Frank nudged him with his elbow.

"We will, Mrs. Ackerman," Frank said. "Thanks."

As they followed Adam's mother, Joe whispered, "Why are we going into the house, Frank?"

"Because Mrs. Ackerman is being nice!" his brother whispered back. "That's why."

"Okay, okay," Joe sighed, "but Adam won't be nice when he sees us again!"

Adam was still on the floor when Frank and Joe entered the den. Tony grunted as he tried prying the Frisbee from one dog's mouth. The hamster, still wearing his space helmet, watched from the stack of books.

"Sorry, Adam," Joe said. "I should know not to throw a Frisbee into the house."

"Or near dogs, genius!" Adam snapped as he stood up. "You know how they get around Frisbees!"

Adam dusted powdered sugar off his shirt. "And what's with all this sugar on your Frisbee? I look like a jelly doughnut."

"It's part of Frank's project for the science fair," Joe said. "Tell him about it, Frank. . . . Frank?"

Joe looked around the room for his brother. He

found Frank facing the computer. Joe looked over Frank's shoulder. On the screen there was a picture of a hamster in outer space!

"This picture is like the others we got," Frank said, "of the hamster traveling through time."

Adam's eyes lit up when he heard about the pictures. He puffed his chest out proudly.

"How did you like the big one on your garage door?" he asked. "I used a special program on my dad's laptop to project the picture hundreds of times its size!"

"So that was you hiding in the hedges," Joe said. "How come we didn't see you?"

"I guess I'm a fast runner," said Adam.

Joe frowned as he recalled Adam running from the lunchroom. "We know that," he said. "You're also fast at something else."

"Oh yeah?" Adam asked. "What?"

Joe pointed to the hamster. "Snatching Crusty out of Phil's time machine—"

"Um, Joe," Frank interrupted.

Joe turned to Frank. "What?"

"That's not Crusty," Frank said. "Crusty has a white spot on his stomach. That hamster doesn't."

Joe looked at the hamster's stomach. Frank was right. No white spot. No Crusty.

"Oh. Okay," Joe said. "Who is he, then?"

"My pet hamster," Tony answered. "His name is Squeaky!"

"I wanted you to think Squeaky was Crusty," Adam told the brothers, "and that he really did travel back in time."

"Ha!" Joe scoffed. "As if I would ever believe that!"

Frank raised an eyebrow at Joe. Seriously?

"Next I was just going to put Squeaky in outer space," Adam said excitedly. "So you would think he was on his way to the future!"

"Why did you do all that, Adam?" asked Frank.

"Because it's fun," Adam said with a shrug. "And I wanted to mess with you."

"That explains the hamster pictures," Joe said. "But it doesn't explain something else."

"What?" Adam asked, annoyed.

"Why did you run out of the lunchroom?" asked Joe.

Adam's face suddenly burned red. "The mist and all those lights on the time machine reminded me of something," he snapped.

"Reminded you of what?" Frank asked.

"I bet it reminded Adam of a creepy Halloween house we went to last week," Tony said, and laughed. "He was so scared, he ran out of that, too. You should have seen him—"

"Zip it, Tony!" Adam cut in.

Frank and Joe traded grins. So Adam hadn't taken Crusty. He was scared of creepy Halloween houses. But that wasn't all they had learned about Adam. . . .

"We didn't know you were so good with computers, Adam," Frank said. "How did you make those pictures?"

"I looked online for pictures of different times in history," Adam explained, "and then I used a special program to make it look like Squeaky was there."

"I took the pictures of Squeaky," said Tony. "It's a good thing Jet Set Pet had teeny Halloween costumes for hamsters."

Adam gazed at his computer and sighed.

"Messing with you Hardys was fun," he admitted. "I'm going to miss making those pictures on the computer."

"Cheer up, Adam," Joe smirked. "I'm sure you'll find other ways to mess with us."

A noise made the boys turn their heads. Squeaky had jumped off the books and was scurrying toward a backpack on the floor.

"Squeaky knows where I stash his food," Tony said, chuckling. "Watch this."

Squeaky squeezed through a small opening, disappearing into Tony's backpack.

"Maybe his name should be Squeezy!" Joe joked.

"Hardy-har-har!" Adam snapped. "And maybe you guys should leave before you crack more stupid jokes."

Frank and Joe smiled at each other. Adam was back to being his old bully self!

"And take your dumb Frisbee with you!" Adam said.

"No, thanks," said Frank. "It's got dog spit all over it."

The brothers left the Ackerman house. On the way home, Joe crossed Adam's name off the suspect list in the clue book.

"Adam thinks he's so tough," Joe said, and laughed. "But now we know he was scared of some goofy Halloween house for kids."

SUSPECTS:

1. ~~Trent~~
2. ~~Adam~~
3. ~~Phil~~

"He is good at something, Joe," Frank pointed out. "Computer photography."

"And Squeaky is great at getting into tight spaces," said Joe. "I wonder if all hamsters are good at that."

Joe was about to close his clue book, when something clicked. . . .

Hamsters? Tight spaces?

"Frank," he said. "Maybe we're wrong."

"Wrong about what?" Frank asked.

"About Crusty," Joe replied. "Maybe he wasn't taken out of Phil's time machine!"

THE HARDY BOYS—and YOU!

→ **YOU!** ←

CAN YOU SOLVE THE MYSTERY OF THE MISSING HAMSTER?

Think like Frank and Joe Hardy to solve the case. Or turn the page to find out what happens next.

1. Frank and Joe have ruled out Trent, Phil, and Adam as suspects. If someone did take Crusty out of the time machine—whodunit? On a sheet of paper, list other possible suspects.

2. Joe thinks Crusty may not have been taken out of Phil's time machine. How else could the hamster have gotten out? Write your answers on a sheet of paper.

3. Frank and Joe each invented detective science projects. If you could invent a detective project for your science fair, what would it be? How would it work? Draw or write your ideas on a sheet of paper.

4. Which clues helped you to solve this mystery? Write them down.

Chapter 10

NICK OF TIME!

"If someone didn't take Crusty out of Phil's time machine, how could he have gotten out?" Frank asked.

"If hamsters can squeeze into and out of tight spaces," Joe explained, "maybe Crusty squeezed out of the time machine."

Joe turned to a fresh page in his clue book. Frank watched as Joe began to doodle.

"What are you drawing?" Frank asked.

"Phil's time machine," Joe answered, "and all the different places Crusty could have escaped from."

He drew arrows pointing under the time machine door and at the air holes.

"We have to see if there's enough room for Crusty to have squeezed out," said Frank. "Let's go to the school and look at Phil's time machine."

"And look for Crusty," Joe added.

Frank and Joe walked the few blocks to Bayport Elementary School. The brothers headed straight to the lunchroom and Phil's time machine. Luckily, the lunchroom was open, and they walked right in.

"There's no room between the time machine and the floor," Frank said as they eyed it from top to bottom.

"Yeah," Joe agreed. "Crusty would have to be as flat as a tortilla to squeeze out underneath."

Frank pointed to the airholes. "He might have squeezed out one of those."

"Let me see," Joe said. He walked around the time machine to the two air holes. But when he looked through—

"Ahhhhhhh!" he shouted. "Two eyes are staring back at meeeeeeee!"

"Who is it?" Frank asked.

"Who do you think it is?" a familiar voice inside the time machine asked. "George Washington?"

"Phil?" Frank and Joe said in unison.

The time machine door opened. Out stepped Phil.

"What were you doing in there?" Joe asked.

"It's my science fair project, remember?" said Phil. "I wanted to figure out how to make it more like a time machine. Like Ms. Klinger told me to."

"We were trying to figure out something too," Frank said. "How Crusty could have escaped on his own."

"You think he escaped?" Phil repeated.

"We think he might have squeezed out through one of the air holes," Joe said. "That is, if he could reach them."

"I built a small shelf underneath the air holes," Phil said. "Crusty could have jumped from the stool to the shelf, then out a hole."

Frank and Joe looked inside the time machine to see for themselves. It was an easy escape route for a hamster.

"If that's how Crusty got out," Frank said, looking around the lunchroom, "where did he go?"

"Maybe he ran into Mrs. Carmichael's kitchen," Phil said, "for some veggies or whatever hamsters like."

"Chet's hamster likes pizza!" Joe said, and chuckled.

Frank smiled too, until he was struck by a thought. "Isn't Chet's science project a slice of pizza?" he asked.

"Yeah!" Joe said excitedly. "And Crusty loves pizza, so—"

"So what are we waiting for?" Frank said. "Next stop—pizza project!"

Frank, Joe, and Phil raced to the table holding Chet's pizza slice. It was still covered with the metal dome-shaped lid.

"How could Crusty get under that thing?" Phil asked. "It's a tight fit."

Joe pointed at a round hole at the top of the dome. "Unless," he said, "Crusty squeezed through this!"

Leaning over, Joe looked down through the hole. "What do you see, Joe?" Frank asked.

"I spy with my little eye," said Joe, "a very full hamster!" He smiled as he pulled off the cover.

"Crusty!" Frank and Phil cried.

The little hamster sat next to the pizza slice. His cheeks were stuffed as he nibbled on the crust.

"And look," Joe said, pointing to the hamster's pizza-filled stomach. "White marks the spot. It's Crusty, you guys!"

"This is awesome," Phil said. "Wait until we tell Chet that we found Crusty!"

"You found Crusty?" a voice asked.

The three boys turned to see Chet. Their friend was wearing a white baker's hat and apron streaked with blue and yellow frosting.

"Well?" Chet asked. "Where's my hamster?"

Joe stepped aside to reveal Crusty. "Ta-daaa!" he announced. "There he is—living up to his name!"

When Chet saw Crusty, he smiled from ear to ear. "At least the crust isn't moldy yet," he said. "Stale, but not moldy."

"What are you doing at school today, Chet?" Frank asked. "And why are you dressed like a chef?"

"My cake decorating club meets here every Sunday," Chet said. "I get to eat whatever I decorate. Good deal."

He picked up his hamster. "How did you find Crusty anyway?" he asked.

"Hamsters squeeze out of tight spaces," Frank explained. "That's how he got out of his carrier on Friday. And out of Phil's time machine."

Chet turned to Phil. "Sorry I blamed you," he said. "I just wanted my hamster back. So did Iola."

"It's cool," Phil said. "I'm just glad Crusty didn't go back in time. That would have been weird."

"And kind of awesome," Joe admitted.

Phil heaved a big sigh. "You know what's not awesome?" he asked. "The science fair is tomorrow, and I still don't know how to make my time machine more like a time machine!"

Joe looked across the lunchroom at Phil's science project. It was built really well. Maybe it just needed more lights. Or pink mist. Or . . . something else!

"How about pictures of different times in history flashing on and off?" Joe asked Phil. "All over the outside of your time machine?"

"Sounds neat," Phil said. "But how am I going to do that?"

Joe thought of the pictures of Squeaky and smiled. "Don't worry, Phil," he said. "I know just the guy for the job!"

On Monday the Bayport Elementary School Science Fair was in full swing. Lots of kids tried on Joe's lie detector helmet. And Frank demonstrated his fingerprint project on the principal himself!

But the project that drew the biggest crowd was Phil's time machine, with its picture tour of the world through history.

"The Phil and Adam Time Warp Wonder is a hit!" Joe said as he and Frank watched it from across the lunchroom.

"What's really a wonder is that Adam can stop being a bully for a day," Frank said, "and do something good."

"Yeah," Joe said with a grin. "And it's about TIME!"

Looking for another great book?
Find it
IN THE MIDDLE.

Fun, fantastic books for kids
in the in-be**TWEEN** age.

IntheMiddleBooks.com

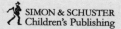
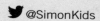

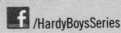

Nancy Drew

★ CLUE BOOK ★

Test your detective skills with
Nancy and her best friends,
Bess and George!

NancyDrew.com

Join Zeus and his friends as they set off on the adventure of a lifetime.

Now Available:

HEROES IN TRAINING
Perseus and the Monstrous Medusa
Joan Holub & Suzanne Williams